# Dana: A Dangerous Connection

Jonnie Patterson

# Dana: A Dangerous Connection

## Author

*Jonnie Patterson*

## Editor

*McBright*

## Illustrator

*Ishika Sharma*

# Dedication

This book is dedicated to all my Guardian Angels in heaven looking down, but especially my God brother Trince Thibeadeaux. Thanks for always believing in me. I love you to the moon and back, big brother.

# INTRODUCTION

Money, drugs, and a new plug, these brothers thought they had it all. Body and Bun was living life in the fast lane with their CMM clique until things spun out of control quickly. The men needed help to get their drug empire back on the right track and they found it from a total stranger, Dana. They are asking a lot from a person they don't know. Will she come through for the brothers? Or will she prove to be another problem in their master plan? Join the brothers as they make a new friend and find out who is really in their corner and who's in their business.

# Chapter One

## One Call

"Nigga the connect taking a liking to ya boi," Ace said while getting comfortable inside Body's 2014 all black Chevy Tahoe. The interior was a mix of black and grey. So, as soon as Body pulled away from the busy airport, the inside of the vehicle was immediately swept with darkness. The two men exit the airport and into Lafayette traffic, stopping to a light before getting on to Highway 90 in the direction of Broussard to handle some business that Body set up.

"We got packages coming in later this week bro. We still the one stop shop with the exclusive Pedro. Aww yeah my boi, we got that gas for they ass," Ace said in reference to the new weed they had received from their supplier while he reached for the radio dial to change the music.

Body was into southern rappers such as Z-Ro, Kevin Gates, Bun B, Boosie and others, while Ace preferred a wide range of music. He even enjoyed rapping himself.

"What he sending that shit in this time? I hope it's some shit I can use this time," Body said while giving Ace the side eye for messing with his radio.

"That nigga said some dog food or dog treats."

"What the fuck I'ma do with dog food?"Body queried

"Donate it! You worried about the wrong shit nigga."

"You funny my nigga, So, what you mean the plug taking a liking to you son?"

"This that nigga, Bishop, second time sending me straight to the plug to set up my shipments. So picture me and the plug chopping it up and that nigga was on some maybe we should cut out the middle man and deal just between us. That nigga told me he was gonna hit my line with specifics and everything,"Ace said

"Why that nigga Bishop stop setting you up with one of his bitches to make your shipments and drop offs?"

"Because every time he set that shit up, I send that hoe back weak and beat."

"Nigga, what?"

"I fuck'em."

"Boi, you wild for that."

"Looked like that shit worked out in our favor though."

"Bet."

"Did you check with that nigga Bun to make sure that nigga got shit lined up so we can get this weight distributed in these streets?"

"We bout to pull up on that nigga now"

"What the fuck we going there for?"

"We got business to discuss son."

Body turned the corner into a neighborhood with beautiful brick homes on one side of the street and an apartment complex on the other side. The apartment complex was surrounded by trees. Even in the darkness of the night it was easy to tell the complex was a very peaceful and clean place to stay. Every apartment had matching brown balconies, red doors, and gold lanterns for porch lights. Body turned into the last drive way and parked in the first spot.

Body and Ace exit the vehicle and walked over to Bun's apartment. After knocking on the red door with the black numbers 265 painted on it, Bun opened the door wearing only some basketball shorts. His six pack abs greeted Body and Ace at the same time he did. Body and Ace walked pass Bun like they were not visiting his house, but rather lived there. Body immediately reached for the white T-shirt that rested on Bun's oversized black leather sectional sofa, and throws it at Bun.

Bun's apartment was the true definition of a bachelors pad. He had a Scarface theme going throughout his apartment with everything being either black, red, or gold. Every piece of furniture was oversized, which made the massive apartment seem smaller. He finished off his theme with an oversized picture of the water fountain that was in Tony Montana's house with the inscription "The World is Yours" hanging over his oversized leather sofa.

The three men gathered on the sofa and began to discuss their next move for the products they were going to receive. Shortly into the conversation,

Ace's phone rings, he pulls it out of his pocket and swipes up to accept and answered the phone.

"Whoa." Ace said while getting up from the sofa to take his phone call outside while Body and Bun continued their discussion.

"What's good who dis?" Ace said as he did not recognize the number when he answered the phone.

"This your new connect people delivering a message from Julio. He wants you guys to pick up shipment that was intended for you guys and someone else. The shipment is hot, but one of our people intercepted and got it ducked off. It needs to be moved now. If you and your people can handle that, then consider yourself part of the team."

"Me and my people on that shit."

"I will send the details shortly."

"Say less," Ace said and ended the call and walked back into Bun's apartment.

"Say I hate to fuck up you'll conversation but the plug want us to go on a trial run and pick up our packages that was intercepted," Ace said while standing in front of the TV.

"Where we gotta go get this shit from?"

"Shit, I don't know. I waiting for the plug people to drop the location," Ace said while his phone chimed in the background to alert him of a notification. Ace pulled his phone out of his pocket and quickly read the text message that came from a number that was not saved in his phone.

"Shit looks like we going to Houston. We gotta go with our move quick are miss our opportunity to work with Julio, " Ace said while showing Body and Bun the address of where they were supposed to pick up their package.

"We gonna heading out that way tomorrow night. A quick in and out trip. I guess we can bring that nigga Des with us so we can start training that nigga. With all this work we moving we, gonna need some more foot soldiers."

"Bet."

# Chapter 2

## Bloody Trail

Body maneuvered his all black 2014 Chevy Tahoe through Houston's Friday night traffic. He was very excited to travel back to Louisiana to load the streets with his new products that came from Cali, Mexico, and Colorado. Body and Ace knew since they had successfully completed the pick up that they were now in a very powerful partnership with the most notorious King Pin in the south. Both men knew the meaning of this connection and knew that they would be cutting out long time middle man, Bishop. Bishop always gave them stepped on product which would bring in less profit, but now the opportunity to step up their game was in the trunk of Body's SUV.

While emerging on the highway, Body started to put his plan into motion by bouncing ideas off Ace and Des. The amount of products they were about to distribute was way more than they were used to. So, their distribution methods would have to be totally different. The men would be introducing a variety of marijuana, cocaine, and pills into the streets.

"Nigga we gotta move this work fast; ol'boy mention we got a shipment of this size coming in in less than a week," Body said mentioning one of Julio people that was there at the pickup who mentioned that their regular shipment would not be affected by this pick up. Ace did not stop his freestyle, but paid close attention to what Body said.

Body, Bun, Ace and all their siblings grew up together in the same public housing. Their mothers were best friends and Body and Bun's dad was even cousins to Ace's mother. Ever since toddlers, the three boys were inseparable. They often referred to each other as brothers and no one could tell them anything different.

Ace was 5'7" with a caramel complexion, straight pearly white teeth, slight slants to his dark brown eyes, and an athletic built frame. For a guy his size, he was abnormally strong, fast, and could eat his body weight in food. His personality stood out, he would make anyone laugh, any woman feel beautiful, and could sell ice to a polar bear.

Ace, Body, and Bun always worked well together, if Ace was not clowning Body about his height. Bun was the enforcer, Body was the muscle, and Ace was the speed. Together they were the brains. They had been introduced into the game since they were teenagers and now they are messing with a boss in the game.

Ace stopped mid rap lyric to voice his opinion on the sales of their new products. "The streets dry as fuck. So we should have no problems with feeding the birds and collecting the bread." Ace took a glance at the back seat were Des was seated.

"Nigga, you still texting? Leave ya bitch alone, the way Body drive we will be back in The Boot real quick."

Ace pulled out a pack of Swisher Diamonds from his pants pocket.

"Time to test the product fam, and also celebrate our new foot soldier. Welcome to CMM, Des."

The three men put a blunt of Cali exclusive in the air, while Ace confirmed Des' induction into the CMM, Cashay Money Movement, family.

Des was one of Money friends that always hung around waiting for his opportunity to be put in the game. This was finally his time to show them why he was worthy of being part of the money-making movement.

Body swung the heavy Chevy through Houston traffic while Ace went between rapping to teaching Des the ends and outs of being a valuable foot soldier. Des continued to text as Ace put him on game as Body was almost clear of the Friday night traffic jam. As Body emerge from the traffic, he notice that there was two dark colored cars that may have been following him. He decided that he would jump on the Sam Houston Toll way since it was less crowded to see if he was indeed being followed.

Body entered the highway and rode the middle lane as he always did. Shortly after entering the highway, his suspicion was confirmed when the two dark colored old school impalas trailed him onto the toll way, one riding the left lane and one riding the right lane. Body did not hesitate to reach for his gun under his seat and place it onto his lap. Ace quickly caught on after he noticed Body place his gun onto his lap and reached for his gun that was inside of his bag on the passenger side floor. Des was not far behind as he pulled his gun out of his waistline.

The dark colored Impala's were now just ahead of them. Body began to speed up in an effort to pass them up, but the vehicles held their position. The Toll way was lit up by street lights but none of the men could manage to see inside the vehicles.

The men became anxious as they anticipated the next move from suspicious vehicles. They did not wait too long, the car in the left lane swerved over into Body's lane causing Body to swerve over to the right towards the closest exit ramp. The car on the right maneuvered in a manner to guide Body's SUV off the highway and onto a not-so-busy and dark service road.

While exiting off onto the service road, the car in the left lane side swiped the driver's side of Body's SUV causing it to spin and flip onto its side. The two cars came to a stop immediately in front of the overturned SUV and out of the two vehicles exit men dressed in all black with black ski masks on their faces. The masked men surrounded the overturned vehicle with guns drawn. They were greeted by an assortment of bullets coming from Body's SUV.

The masked men returned fire aiming in the direction from which the bullets were coming.

"Des, what the fuck you doing still in the truck? Grab the bags and bring your stupid ass on," One of the masked men screamed over the gun fire.

The shower of bullets came to an end as Des began to exit the SUV with two duffle bags. He handed them off to one of the masked men as blood dripped from his bullet wound to his left shoulder. Des joined the men as they ran to their cars and took off into the night leaving their dead and wounded on the street.

Body clung to life as he felt death-gripping pain all over his body. He tried to move his legs, but the pains only worsen when he tried to move. He looked toward the passenger seat and saw Ace's lifeless body slumped against the window. He could hear sirens in the background, but that did not stop him from yelling out for help. Body held onto his cousin, Ace, and screamed for help until his surroundings slowly started to fade away.

# Chapter 3

## Awaken

**POW! POW!**

Body awakened from a deep sleep. He instantly passed his hands over his body and noticed an IV connected to his left hand and a blood pressure cuff on his right arm. There were sticky pads attached to his chest with wires coming from them and a constant beeping noise coming from a machine on a stand nearby. Body knew he was indeed in a hospital, but he was not sure how he got there or how long he has been there.

"By time ya big ass did something other than sleep. I been here over a week strong waiting to see if you had other tricks up your sleeve my baw," Body's younger sister Ja'Lynn said.

He instantly felt himself getting annoyed, but those feeling subsided when he noticed her puffy red eyes and her bible resting on her lap.

"A nigga had to get his beauty rest lil sis. Besides, you know they can't keep a real nigga down," Body said while adjusting himself in the tiny hospital bed. He glanced at his baby sister and quickly admired her bronze skin and her young chubby face. Body and Ja'Lynn were like water and oil, but Body loved his sister more than anything.

"I guess it's like Maw-Maw always said you can't kill bad grass," Ja'Lynn said as her big beautiful brown eyes stared down at her open bible.

"Sis, what happened and how long I been in this bitch."

"You and Ace were involved in some street violence on the highway. The cops are saying it's a case of mistaken identity since your truck is almost identical to a well-known King Pin."

Body knew without a shadow of doubt that it was not a mistake, but he would go along with it as long as it meant he was not going to jail. His sister did not mention anything about drugs. So, that means that whatever happened, happened before a pickup or he was robbed.

"What room they have Ace in? I know that nigga giving them nurses hell and eating all them people food," Body said while trying to move his legs, but he was limited because one of his legs was in a cast and the other had a compression device on it that help with circulation to his legs.

Ja'Lynn looked out of the huge window that was directly behind her and said, "Ace is dead, Marlon."

"Girl stop playing! Ja'Lynn, this not a time to play like this, call that nigga phone."

Ja'Lynn turned her baby face to Body, looked him straight in the eyes and repeated herself. "Ace is dead, Marlon. One of the bullets hit him in a main artery."

Body's face fell and his mind went blank. Ace and Body were inseparable. They had been getting into trouble since diapers. This death would be a hard one to get over for Body.

"When is his funeral? I gotta make sure I'm outta this bitch to see my nigga off."

"His service was a few days ago, Marlon. You've been in a medically induced coma for about two weeks now."

Body looked around the room in disbelief as anger took over his body. He knew he had to get out of that hospital and he had to do it fast before he hurt someone. He ripped the IV out of his hand, pulled back the sheets and headed towards the door dragging blood pressure machine and all. Ja'Lynn yelled her brother's name, but there was no stopping him once he was this emotional. All at once, a gang of medical staff stormed the room in an effort to place Body back into his hospital bed.

Body began to swing wildly at the hospital staff as he was desperate to escape his new reality. He knocked over and dragged nurses and doctors alike to get to the exit as one of the nurses signal for another nurse at the nearby nurses station to grab something to calm their patient down.

Ja'Lynn's face was filled with tears as she continued to urge her brother to get back into bed and that he had to focus on getting better. She knew her words were falling on deaf ears because once her brother reached this level of rage, there was no stopping him.

A nurse with a syringe of medication came racing down the hallway in the direction of Body's hospital room. She was right on time because Body was finally working his way out of the room. His back was turned toward the hallway as the gang of hospital staff tugged on Body's arms and shoulders. The nurse with the syringe of medication removed the cap from the needle, put her finger on the plunger, and administered the drug directly into one of Body's ass cheeks that was exposed from the back of his hospital gown. Body felt the sting of the medicine being pushed into his system and immediately swung around. He picked up his massive arm in an effort to swing at the nurse, but instead hit the floor like a ton of bricks.

The medical staff moved the sleeping giant into his bed as Ja'Lynn explained to them why her brother went from being in a coma to becoming the Hulk.

POW! POW!

Body woke up, covered in sweat. His mind went back to the previous events of the day, finding out his cousin was dead, finding out he was in the hospital for over two weeks, and slowly coming to realize he did not know who or what caused all of this. He looked around the moonlit hospital room as one thought consumed him. He would not stop until he found out what happen to his cousin, Ace, and when he finds out who were behind it, they would be as good as dead.

# Chapter 4

## What's the Move

"Body, what the fuck is wrong with you my nigga?" Bun said while he passed stacks of money through a money counter. The two brothers were setting up pickups and drop off of drugs and money from the back room of one of the many Laundromats Body owned.

Body was day dreaming about a revenge plot on how to kill the person that was responsible for the death of his cousin, Ace. It had been months since Body's trip to Houston, in which he had gotten robbed and left for dead. He tried everything in his power to find out who was responsible for the hit that had him grieving the loss of his cousin, Ace.

The streets were abnormally quiet about the entire situation. No one knew anything or was too afraid to say anything.

No matter how Body felt about the loss of Ace, business had to go on and he had to make sure that it was flawless. After getting robbed in Houston for over 100,000 worth of drugs, their plug stayed in business with them partial so they could work off the debt, but mostly because he wanted CMM to tie up the loose ends of their robbery. Julio had a bond with Ace; so finding out who crossed him by stealing his product, became that more personal when he found out Ace was killed in the process. With both Julio and Body's ears to the streets, they were bond to find out something sooner or later.

Body snapped out of his day dream and continued to bag and weigh the various drugs to get them ready for distribution.

"Man what the fuck wrong with you?" Bun asked, while looking directly at his brother's blank stare as he bagged the product.

"Shit still trying to figure out what the fuck happened," Body said, returning his attention on the product he was bagging.

"I know that shit is annoying to not remember what happened to you and Ace. In due time, it will all come to you. But for now, we just have to put that pressure to these niggas in these streets."

"When we find out who did this shit, I'm wiping they whole family off the map, on God."

"Bet"

Body's phone began to vibrate on the white folding table. He immediately recognized the number; he swiped up, picking up the phone. It was their plug, Julio, calling. Body's stomach dropped and he instantly hoped nothing was wrong.

"Whoa"

"Word on the street is Bishop set up the hit in Houston."

"Where you heard that shit from?"

"I have my ears to more than just the streets and you need to tighten shit up in your crew."

"You think one of my people had something to do with this shit? Don't beat around the bush my nigga, come out with that shit so I can handle it."

"All I'm saying is think real hard about what happened that night."

"Don't you think I been doing that shit? I can't remember shit that happened. Do you know who the leak in my crew is?"

"I don't know if anyone from your crew was a part of this, but it makes sense that someone from your clique would have to help Bishop. I know one thing, don't make any stupid decision to react to this news while your emotions are high. Bishop is the only person I know that don't have any men in his circle. Trust me, I want that nigga dead just as bad as you do. I cut that lame off to fuck with real soldiers and this nigga think he just gonna rob me. We gotta be real smart about how to move with this one because knowing Bishop, we may have one shot at this."

"We gonna have to find a female hitta to take this nigga out," Body suggested.

"Pretty much, unless you don't want that nigga dead."

"I want that nigga more than dead, I want his whole existence gone."

"That's what I'm talking about. Call me if you need anything to make this happen, and I mean anything."

The call ended and Body tossed his phone onto the table.

"What that shit was about?" Bun said while placing rubber bands around large stacks of money.

"That nigga said Bishop put the hit out on us."

"That's fucked up my boi. You know what that mean, right?"

"Means we have to put that nigga in the dirt, but we have to do this shit right. I have a strong feeling we may only have one chance to kill this nigga."

"We can send that nigga Reaper to clear that shit out real quick. You know that nigga stay ready with a 100 round drum."

"Bishop a different breed, that nigga only hang with fine ass females. So sending a nigga to take him out wouldn't work, no matter how good of a hitta. We have to find a fine ass female with the heart of a killer to take that nigga out. But were the fuck we suppose to find a bitch like that?"

"Be cool my nigga. We can still use Reaper; he can snatch one of Bishop bitches that Ace was fucking. We gotta do a little homework and find out what bitch gonna flip on that nigga off the strength of Ace."

"See, that's why I keep ya ass around," Body said.

"Get the fuck out of here! You keep me around because I'm the brains of all this shit," Bun boasted.

"Just cause you my big brother don't think I won't whip ya ass."

"Nigga sit your oversize ass down."

"Fuck you bitch."

"Ya moma a bitch."

"Nigga that's your moma too."

"That's how I know she a bitch."

"Boy you sad. So, how soon can we get that nigga Reaper on that mission?"

"It's always business with your ass. We can get him on that shit ASAP. Let me make the call right now.

# Chapter 5

## Reaper

Reaper sat on his 2003 Suzuki GXSR 1000 crotch rocket. The bike was all black, every trim, bolt, light, and every accessory. Reaper was dressed in all black, with a black helmet on with a mirror tent visor. He positioned himself in the shadow of the night on the side of a popular swingers club called *Swing*. The club was literally in the middle of nowhere. Trees, empty fields, and a not-so-busy highway was the only thing surrounding this place. The view from the highway would make anyone think that the building was abandoned from the lack of signage and lights in front of the building. Even when the building was being occupied, it still looked like it was abandoned. Swing had its own rules, all members of the popular swingers club would arrive at a specific time and leave at a set time. There was never anyone walking or hanging out outside the club during business hours, except for the owner and his lady of the evening.

Bishop or his lady would occasionally step out the back of the club where no one could see them to smoke or just to get away from the members.

Reaper was ready to snatch Bishop's girl of the night, Kandi. Kandi was the last female Ace fucked when Bishop set them up to do a pick up. Kandi admired Ace and took it hard when she found out about his death. Ace and Kandi continued to mess around behind Bishop's back even after he stopped Ace from lining up his pick-ups with his women. Kandi was starting to develop deep feelings for Ace when he was killed so suddenly.

Reaper was growing impatient as he began to sweat underneath his helmet. Reaper was used to quick work, like a drive by or sneak attacks. He never liked when Bun would ask him to do a slow drawn out task.

Reaper and Bun had been friends for years. The two men met while working a six month hitch on an offshore rig. Both men were born and raised in Acadiana area of Louisiana and were used to their food being seasoned a certain type of way. The two men met in the cafeteria of the rig; both men shared a dislike of the under-seasoned food.

After their first conversation, Bun could automatically tell that something was off with his co-worker Xavier, but the two men became close anyways. It wasn't until almost the end of their hitch that Bun confirmed his hunch about Xavier was true. While waiting to depart from the rig, Bun and Xavier were in the midst of a conversation of their childhood. Reaper admitted to killing a man he saw rape his mother.

He said that he could hear his mom scream from his room and when he opened her door her boyfriend was punching her as she screamed. They both were naked. He ran to his mothers safety as he attempted to attack the man with is little fist. The strange man pushed a young Xavier off of him so hard that the young boy flew into the nearest wall. Xavier knew his mom kept a gun in a shoe box under her bed so he immediately went for the weapon. Two shots went off, and the strange man fell off the bed onto the floor lifeless.

Bun looked into Xavier's eyes and saw nothing, no emotions. From that moment on, Bun knew Xavier had the heart of a killer. That is the very day and time Reaper was born. Any time Bun needed a quick hit taken care of, he called his boy Reaper. Reaper was always happy to fulfill his request not only because he took pleasure in killing, but because Bun paid him so handsomely.

After sitting in the same spot for almost an hour, Reaper had enough. He was just about to leave when he saw the exit door to the back of the club swing open and smoke fly out followed by a short petite female. From the looks, it was in fact, Kandi. She was sucking hard on the end of a fat blunt as she retrieved her phone out of her bra. From her facial expression, it was obvious she was upset. Kandi was a short woman, only standing five feet even. She was petite, probably weighing no more than 110 pounds. She was the perfect size to grab, toss over the bike, and ride out into the darkness of the night.

Reaper carefully removed himself off of his bike and positioned himself so he was ready to grab her and run. As he watched her, waiting for the right moment, he took in her beautiful features. Her chocolate complexion was still beautiful even in the dark. Her face reminded him of the Bratz doll his little sister played with when they were younger. Kandi had full lips, big beautiful eyes, and a cute button nose. Her natural coils swayed in the breeze. She definitely was a head turning beauty.

Kandi turned in the opposite direction of where Reaper was and started walking in that direction away from the still opened exit door. Reaper knew this was the perfect time to grab and go. He swiftly moved on the cement pavement being careful not to step on anything that would make noise. He approached Kandi, grabbed her, and tossed her over his shoulder. She let out a loud scream and began to kick. He never loosens his grip on her no matter how much she screamed or kicked. He finally reached his bike. He hopped on, dropped Kandi's body over the gas tank, applied his body weight to her, started the bike and was gone out of the parking lot right before Bishop came storming out of the exit to the club. Bishop looked around and could not see anything, but he heard the loud humming from the full Voo Doo exhaust Reaper had on his bike.

Five minutes later, Reaper pulled up to a car junk yard with Kandi still screaming. Reaper helped her get off the bike and then removed his helmet revealing his midnight skin and handsome face. He grabbed Kandi by her shoulders and looked her in her eyes and told her that if she screamed again, he would kill her. Kandi saw no fears or emptiness to his words, so she quickly followed his demands.

"Where are we and what do you want from me? Who are you?" Kandi asked while adjusting her weight in her six inch red bottom pumps.

"All your questions will be answered shortly." Reaper said while putting his phone back into his black jean pocket. Kandi could see two figures getting closer to them. So she began to worry and started walking backwards. Reaper immediately grabbed her by the arms and greeted Bun and Body as they walked up.

Both men extended their hands out to shake Kandi's hand, but she did not return the gesture. The men pulled their hands back while Body introduced himself and everyone in attendance.

"I'm Body, this here is my brother Bun and the nigga on the bike that snatched you up is Reaper. I guess you wondering why you here. Our brother, Ace, fucked with you, so that mean we fuck with you."

The very mention of Ace name brought tears to her eyes. She was falling hard and fast for him and his death hunted her every day.

Kandi's attitude changed immediately.

"I'm guessing by the way you'll grabbed a bitch, you'll mother fuckers feel the same way I do,"

Kandi said while straightening her fitted dress over her petite frame.

"How you feel about what? What you talking about lil baby," Body said while removing his hands out of his pockets.

"What I'm saying is, I feel like Bishop had something to do with Ace's death. I can't prove it, but I know that bitch was mad as hell when his connect drop his ass."

"The hit wasn't a hit on Ace. It was a setup to rob us of our first shipment from the plug. I can't really remember what happened that night, but I know the plug said his people heard Bishop was behind the whole thing with the help of one of my foot soldiers."

"So what you'll need me to do? What the fuck you got me here for because I ain't no killer?"

"Be easy Ma, we not asking you to kill nobody. We asking you to do exactly what you doing right now," Bun said while rubbing his hands together.

"And what exactly is that?"

"Be pretty and keep your eyes on Bishop. All I'm asking is, will you have our back when we need you?"

"Anything for Ace."

"That's what I like to hear. We gonna set you up with a lil trap phone and when we need you, expect that phone call with the details of your assignment. If you hear anything about the bitch in our crew that help set that bull shit up press and hold five on the phone and it will automatically call my burner."

"Say less. Now somebody bring me back, and please not this midnight nigga on this death trap."

Bun and Body both laughed, while Reaper shot his middle finger in Kandi's direction. Bun dropped Kandi back on the side of the club, and before he left, reminded her of their plans and handed her a black flip phone which she placed inside her bra. Kandi walked into the back exit door and closed the door. Shortly after entering the club and walking past the restroom, Kandi was thrown hard against the wall. She was face to face with Bishop.

"Where the fuck were you?" Bishop said while he held a firm grip onto Kandi's arms.

"I've been here supervising shit dummy!" Kandi said knowing if he felt like she was lying he would kill her right where she stood.

"You lying bitch, I heard you scream bitch. I went outside and didn't see ya ass nowhere. So where the fuck were you?"

"Look nigga, I went outside to smoke a blunt and I seen one of them big ass rats that I told ya dumb ass be around here. I screamed and came my ass right back in the club. Them fucking rats better security then them security guards. Your selfish ass must have taken your forever to see why I was screaming."

"I told you them rats not gonna do your ass shit, stop screaming like you crazy."

"Well, send Master Splinter people packing and I won't have a reason to scream."

"Bitch, you lucky ya ass fine, otherwise I would punch you in your shit with ya smart ass mouth."

"Yea, whatever," Kandi said while getting out of Bishop's grasp and walking right past him.

"It's about time for them freaks to go home, so you can come lick my pussy, fuck boy."

"Bring that bitch here. I'll suck the soul outcha ass," Bishop said while following Kandi like a puppy.

# Chapter 6

## A New Friend

"Where the fuck we gonna find a female hitta at? This shit about to be impossible for real my nigga," Body said while removing packages of drugs from inside of laundry detergent containers.

"I think this shit gonna be easier then we think," Bun said while weighing each package and stacking them with the piles that matched.

Bun and Body were in the office part of a small building that Body stored material for the multiple businesses he owned.

"You always so calm on some shit, but how many fine ass female hittas you know? Don't worry, I'ma wait?"

Bun was silent.

"That's what I thought. So, how the fuck this gonna be easy my boi?"

"Be easy lil bro. I'm telling you this shit will work itself out."

"Whatever you say, my dude."

For the next few weeks, Body found himself either communicating with Kandi about the ins and outs of Bishop's operation or doing his own tryouts for a hit woman. Body needed to find a woman pretty enough to catch Bishop's eyes, but was cold hearted and smart enough to not get emotionally attached and carry out the hit.

The search for the perfect female was becoming a full time job and every time he came into communication with Kandi, he knew his window of opportunity was getting smaller and smaller. He knew if he did not find someone or train someone soon, he could lose his chance to avenge his brother, Ace.

Body was switching lanes in his hunter green Dodge Challenger listening to *Middle Child* by J. Cole. He was trying to brush off the disappointment he had from what he thought would have been the perfect hitter. He spent a whole week hanging out with Kior. Kior used to help him move weight from time to time. Body thought she was built Ford-tough, but found out she was softer than baby shit when he approached her on some killer shit.

Body let the music take his mind away from his worries and began to pick up speed and switch lanes on Highway 90 going in the direction of his house in Broussard.

It was early February and besides trying to carry out his plans to take out Bishop, he had to deal with his regular business. Income tax season, which was also Mardi Gras season in Louisiana, was the biggest opportunity to move and sell dope. For years, Body, Bun, and Ace would move dope under the cover of Mardi Gras festivity and ever since he brought it up to his new plug, the same plan fell into action for this year. Body was now being stressed by two problems he had, moving weight and finding a fine ass female killer.

While stopped at a traffic light at the intersection of Highway 90 and Kaliste Saloom, Body spotted a curvy woman walking on the side of the road. She was traveling in the same direction as him. The traffic light turned green and traffic began to flow, he approach the woman and immediately pulled over. He admired her thick frame as her hips swayed as she walked. He continued to ride slowly beside her. As she walked, he rolled his window down.

"Damn you must be tired dragging that slug shorty. You need a ride somewhere?" Body said talking to the lady walking on the side of the highway.

"What the hell you talking about?" The beautiful woman turned around and said.

There was a quick silence between the two in which Body took in the woman's features, from her beautiful brown loose curly hair to her slanted green eyes and her high cheek bones. She was bright like the sun with curves that would make any person, man or woman, look twice. When he looked into her eyes, they gave him the vibe she was not to be fucked with. Body was sure she was checking him out too by the way she slightly bit her bottom lip. The silence was broken when Body gave an answer to her question.

"I'm talking about that ass you dragging back there. You lost or something? I damn sure never seen you around here before. I know damn well you not running from a nigga because you look like you can handle your own. So, what's up with it Ma?"

"Man, look, my ride dipped on me, and I'm not from here. So, basically I'm stuck. I usually don't fuck with people I don't know, but you fine as fuck. So, I'll take you up on that offer."

The young lady opened the passenger side door, sat in the car, and closed the door. Body carefully merged back into traffic.

"What am I supposed to call you?"

"Shit you can call me, 'your nigga' are 'Daddy' are call me what everyone else calls me, Body."

"That's what your mom named you?"

"No, she named me Marlon, but my people call me Body. If you like, I can set you up in my guest room at my crib until you get yourself situated."

The short ride between where he met the beautiful young lady and his house, Body learned the young lady's name and he also told her about an opportunity to put money in her pocket. The young lady, Dana, seemed to be interested, but did not give him an answer as to if she wanted the opportunity or not.

Body set up Dana in his guest room, gave her his number and left her to get some rest.

Body was awakened the next morning by his phone ringing. It was a weird number calling, but he answered anyways. It was Dana, she was willing to help him move product in exchange for him helping her locate her family. Body happily agreed to that and ended the call.

After Dana completed her first task with Body which was picking up packages off of Mardi Gras floats in a small town parade. Body sent Bun and Dana to Texas to deliver the packages and collect payment. It was like killing two birds with one stone, since they also found out Dana's family lived within hours of the drop off spot.

# Chapter 7

# Action

Traveling with Dana was interesting for Bun and it also gave him a new respect for her, not only as a woman but as a killer. Alissa and Dana had done something they had never done before; they let someone in on the truth about the abuse Alissa suffered and why she created Dana.

Dana was dangerous, to say the lease, the way she handled the men who tried to rob her and Bun after their drop was savage; but watching Dana walk from her burning family house covered in blood, emotionless, was very much an eye opener and a turn on to Bun. He never saw a woman filled with so much rage that she could kill with no remorse. She started the car and drove away from the house that was now engulfed with flames like she was leaving her job. He knew right then and there she was just what they needed to take Bishop out.

Body picked up his phone and saw that it was not only 2:30 am but he had a text from his brother Bun.

"I think we found our new hitta," Body read the text message from Bun once more, as he sat up in his king-size bed.

He could finally put his plan into action when it came to knocking off Bishop. Body could not wait to catch up with Bun when he return from Texas with Dana. Body could barely control his excitement as he waited for Bun and Dana to pull up to the drop off point, which was at his warehouse.

Bun and Dana pulled up and exit the car. Body gave Dana a quick look over and admired her beauty as she stood before him in a fitted black dress and six inch pumps. He looked her in her eyes and saw emptiness and immediately felt like she had been through a lot mentally and physically. Body quickly put those thoughts to the side and got straight to business.

As excitement wore off Body, he began to notice blood splatter on Dana's face, body, and hands. He also noticed that she smelled a lot like burning wood. He quickly dismissed the conversation about business to send Dana home to shower and burn her clothing.

Dana did not protest Body's demand; she was gone as soon as the words left Body's mouth. She hopped in the rented car and drove away.

"What happened?" Body asked Bun

"Man too much to discuss, but what I do know is that woman been through a lot and she the true definition of crazy." Bun said while pulling stacks of money out of a black duffle bag and putting them onto a white folding table.

"It's always them fine ones that's crazy, my nigga. I bet she got that smoke," Body said while helping Bun empty the duffle bag.

"Look where ya head at my baw! Bro we gotta be careful with Dana or Alissa whatever she wanna be called," Bun said.

"Who the fuck is Alissa?"

"Dana is Alissa and Alissa is Dana. Is two of them living in that body, my dude."

"Wayyyyy, I know you fucking lying! That mean she give good head, I bet she a freak."

"Baw you wild, we gotta be careful not to cross her because I'm telling you she ruthless. Speaking of crossing, a couple of jack boys ran up on us leaving the spot. Guess who one of them was, Des?"

When Body heard Des' name, he instantly became light headed and hurried to sit on one of the folding chairs that was at the table.

Bun immediately rushed to his brother's side as memories flooded Body's mind about that night he lost his cousin, Ace.

"Des," Body said as his hazel eyes held a blank stare.

"What about Des?" Bun queried while he looked over Body.

"That nigga Des was with us the night Ace was killed. I can't remember everything, but I specifically remember one of the niggas telling that bitch ass nigga, Des to grab the bags and come on. That nigga Des set us up! If what Julio saying about Bishop being behind the hit is true then that nigga Des was working with Bishop. I want that Des' head," Body said while slamming his massive fist onto the table sending stacks of money flying.

"Too late for that. We left that nigga stinking across state lines," Bun said while giving Body a look of disbelief.

"I bet all this shit over us taking that nigga plug and Ace fucking his bitches, especially his head hoe, Kandi."

"Don't worry about all that shit nigga cause now, we got all the shit we need to fuck clean over that bitch. That nigga don't know we got his bitch in our back pocket and that we killed his runner. He don't even know that we know he was behind the robbery that led to Ace's death."

"Fucking right, I knew I loved ya ass for a reason. We can play all that shit in our favor," Body said.

"Yea, now send a bird and let the streets know we got hit across state lines. At the same time, set up Kandi and Dana so that Kandi can teach Dana the game. Bishop gonna be busy tryna find Des ass he not gonna notice a new bitch until it's too late."

"You a real one my nigga."

"Na, nigga you just slow as fuck. You always have been ever since they dropped you on your head as a baby," Bun teased.

"Man fuck you nigga. Why you never tried to catch me?"

"I wanted to see that shit."

"You a whole bitch, outcha."

"Send the bird nigga and shut up."

"Bet."

# Chapter 8

## Go with the Move

Kior found herself needing Body's help as her pockets were on the low side. She knew she had disappointed him by not being down with what he wanted her to do. She wasn't built to be a killer, but with a body like hers, she was built to be a hoe to Body for a night. After all, a girl had to secure her bag by any means necessary.

"You want me to forgive you?" Body said as he grabbed a handful of Kior's ass.

"Yea Daddy." Kior said while twerking her big round ass in Body's face.

"You not working hard enough Ma."

"I know right, but by the end of the night you'll be saying more then you forgive me."

"Is that right?" Body said as he smacked Kior's right ass cheek.

Kior let out a giggle, stopped twerking, faced Body and dropped to her knees. She passed her hands over the growing bulge in Body's pants and finds her way to the button on Body's dark wash Polo jeans. She worked diligently to remove his rock hard dick out of his pants. Kior looked up at him and said, "I can show you better than I can tell you."

Kior took him into her mouth and looked up as she watched Body's eyes roll to the back of his head as she tried her hardest to fit all of him into her mouth. Her throat muscles began to tighten around him as she attempted to work her way to the base of Body's dick. Body was in heaven. Kior's head game always sent chills up his spine. That's why she was saved in his phone as the *Soul Snatcher*.

Kior was putting in overtime pulling all her tricks out to make sure Body would forgive her; she began to slurp, spit, gag, and twirl her tongue on Body's dick as the two were interrupted by the sound of Body's phone ringing.

Body's soul re-entered his body as his phone continued to ring. He reached inside his pocket, retrieved the phone to see it was Bishop's name on his screen.

"A nigga even get his dick suck in peace," Body said out loud while accepting the phone call. Kior went back to what she was doing just at a slower pace. Body struggled to find the right words as Kior's tongue and lips found all the right spots.

"What up with it, Bishop?"

"My nigga, I heard they ran up on ya people. You know who did that bitch ass shit?"

"Na fam, but I got my ears to the streets."

"Shit I took a lost too fam, but what's business without a little lost?"

"Right, Right my nigga. You need something because I'm kind of busy at the moment?" Body said while Kior sat him down on her queen size bed and got in position to do the reverse cowgirl. She grabbed hold of Body's dick and slowly guided into her tight wet pussy as Body grabbed her ass cheek hard.

"Well, shit, I'll make it quick since you too busy for ya boy."

"Awwww…hurry up my nigga," Body said as Kior began to bounce her ass.

"I'm looking for a nigga named Des. Do you know who I'm talking about, that lil nigga been giving my main bitch little sister a hard time, beating on her and shit? I been trying to let that bitch make it but now he interrupting my peace, so now I gotta put my hands on him. I want that lil nigga head. Can you find that nigga for me?"

"That's not a problem my brother. I know exactly who you talking about. I'll hit ya line when I find him."

"Bet."

"Say less," Body said before ending the call.

"Bounce that ass fa me, lil baby," Body told Kior while smacking her left ass cheek and watching her ass jiggle. Kior happily obeyed and gyrated her hips, and bounced up and down to a steady rhythm until Body gripped her hips to remove her from his dick and emptied his load on her waiting ass.

Once the two were done with their sexual encounter, Kior was forgiven for her wrong doings and Body went on home so he could put his plan into action. Kandi had been schooling Dana for almost a week and Body was hoping Dana was a quick leaner because it was time to go with their move on Bishop. Body picked up his phone and called Bun. After two rings, Bun answered.

"Whoa"

Body sat in his car in front of his house as he spoke to his brother about the conversation he had with Bishop.

"That nigga fell right into our trap. He looking for Des and probably thinks Des ran off with the shit he was supposed to take from us."

"I knew that nigga was gonna fall for that shit. Did you check on Kandi and Dana? Kandi needs to introduce Dana to Bishop now while this nigga on the hunt for Des. One thing I know about most niggas, they will stop just about anything to be in the presence of a stallion."

"On God."

"Well my baw, it's time to get your ass to work," Bun said and then hung up in Body's face.

# Chapter 9

# Dana

"Bishop, come here. I got something for you."
Kandi yelled while motioning Dana to have a seat
on the queen size bed in the center of the dim lit
room.

The room was all red and black. The walls were
painted a crimson red with a black ceiling and
matching carpet on the floor. The gold chandelier
that hung over the bed was decorated with black
jewels; it was actually very beautiful but did not
successfully provide much light to the room. The
bed was centered in the room with an oversized
red velvet material head board and black silk
linens.

Dana sat at the edge of the foot of the bed facing
the doorway where Kandi was standing. She was a

little numb because she really did not know what to expect as she did her part in setting Bishop up. Dana had been alone through this all; Alissa was nowhere to be found ever since Kandi and Dana became close.

Dana attempted to take her mind off ending Bishop's life by admiring Kandi's petite frame as she stepped aside for Bishop to enter the room. Bishop stopped just a few steps into the room and licked his lips as he rubbed his hands together.

Dana was slightly turned on by Bishop; he was about five feet ten inches, with cinnamon colored skin and he was thick with much defined muscle tone. His facial features reminded her of the rapper, Da Baby. Dana knew by the way Bishop was eyeing her that he liked what he saw. So, she decided to have a little fun and tease him by being a little extra.

Dana stood up and straightened her five feet six inch frame. Bishop's eyes traveled down Dana's curvy body taking all of her in from head to toe.

"You like what you see?" Dana said while taking a step closer to Bishop.

"Hell yeah, I love what I see. Kandi, you did ya thing on this one," Bishop said while matching Dana's effort by stepping closer to her without taking his eyes off of her.

"I didn't taste her yet, Daddy. I was saving her for you," Kandi said with a smile on her face while she leans against the frame of the door.

"Good girl," Bishop said.

Bishop and Dana were now chest to chest. Bishop already had his hands full of Dana's ass and was planting kisses on her neck as Dana head fell back in pleasure. As soon as Bishop's hands grabbed for the button to Dana's pants, Dana pushed away.

Bishop was not used to not having his way, especially when it came to women. So, Dana's action immediately caused anger to build up inside Bishop, but he was also intoxicated by her presence and wanted more of her. So, he let it slide.

"What's wrong Ma?" Bishop asked as he reached for the button on her pants again.

"The name is Dana, and I'm you'll guess let me see how you'll get down. Kandi, let me see this head game you been talking so much shit about," Dana said while she moved Bishop's hand from her pants.

"You got the game fucked up lil baby; you don't run shit behind these four walls, this all me baby!" Bishop said while tapping his chest with his hand that was just trying to unbutton Dana's pants.

Dana was unfazed by Bishop's display of masculinity as she had a seat on the bed and said,

"Not tonight, you don't run shit around here! Now be easy and let me and my bitch get you right."

It was clear to Bishop that Dana was not from this area or didn't care about his reputation. He couldn't help but to smile, even though he was heated and wanted to put his hands on Dana.

Dana could see the tension in Bishop's face, so she stood up and with her face just inches away from Bishop's face, she brushed her lips against his and said, "I promise I won't disappoint you. Now, be cool."

Dana gently pushed Bishop against the wall and held a hand out in Kandi's direction without taking her eyes off Bishop. Kandi slowly approached the two and placed a hand on the small of Dana's back. Dana grabbed a handful of Kandi's hair and kissed her passionately while massaging her breast with her available hand. All the senses in Kandi awaken as she genuinely enjoyed Dana's touch, taste, and smell. The women were enjoying themselves so much that they didn't even notice when Bishop came out of his pants and began stroking his manhood.

Dana glanced at Bishop, broke her connection with Kandi to address Bishop. "Don't get too excited, we not to the good part yet," Dana said while putting a hand on Bishop's rock-hard dick and stroking it while her other hand that rested on Kandi's shoulder pushed her down toward the floor.

Dana looked down at Kandi as she kneeled directly in front of Bishop and said, "Now, open wide and show me how I'm supposed to suck a dick."

Kandi obeyed Dana's demands by opening her mouth and taking Bishop into her mouth inch by inch. She slowly took him into her mouth until she could not take any more of his massive manhood. She began to tighten her throat muscles around his swollen head and began to bob her head making herself gag on Bishop's dick. Bishop's eyes rolled back as he rested his head up against the wall. As she increased her speed and the messier her head game became, she could feel Bishop's knees get weak.

Dana sat on the bed and enjoyed Kandi pleasing Bishop. She was not holding back on Bishop; she slurped, gagged, spit and choked on Bishop's dick. Bishop could no longer hold his composure and began to moan and squirm on the wall; he even grabbed the back of Kandi's head. Dana took full advantage of Bishop's pleasure, removed her phone from her bra and sent a quick message before removing her clothing and placing them in the corner, on top of her phone.

Dana could tell that Kandi's work was just about over by the way Bishop was now aggressively ramming his dick inside Kandi's mouth. Dana grabbed a handful of Kandi's hair and pulled her upwards. Kandi had a look of relief on her face as she stood up. Dana wasted no time tasting Bishop from Kandi's mouth by sticking her tongue deep into Kandi's mouth.

Anger grew inside of Bishop but it slowly subsided when he noticed a naked Dana was standing in front of him kissing Kandi passionately. Bishop's hands explored Dana's body until he found her wet center; he was pleasantly surprised by her wetness as he began to massage her clit. Dana disconnected her lips from Kandi's and let out a quiet moan.

Dana began to melt as Bishop explored her womanhood. In the back of her head, the thought of killing this man lingered which stopped her from getting too comfortable and lose focus of her true mission, which was to end Bishop's existence.

# Chapter 10

## Put in Work

Hidden by the dark of night, Body, Bun, and a couple of foot soldiers from CMM sat inside a dark blue cargo van. The men were parked on the bank of Bayou Teche directly across from an abandoned ice factory. Body's patience was wearing thin as he waited for a heavily anticipated text from Dana that would give him the green light to bust down the doors on the abandon factory, Bishop's stash spot.

Bun was becoming increasingly angry as Body showed more signs of his patience being limited for their tasked at hand.

"My baw, you really need to be cool with all that moving ya big ass, shaking the van," Bun said looking in the driver side were Body sat.

"Fuck what you talking about, where the fuck is Dana? I thought we would have heard back from her by now," Body said while shifting his weight in the driver's seat.

"Nigga, it's only been thirty minutes! Chill the fuck out!" Bun said while resuming his game of Candy Crush on his smart phone.

The van was consumed with silence which was short lived as Body let his frustration out by letting out a long and loud groan. At the same time, his phone ding alerting him of a new text message he received.

"Do ya thing, he gonna be busy all night," The text message read from Dana.

This old ice factory was Bishop's number one stash spots, clearing this spot out was a big part of their plan. Between Bun, Body, Kandi, and Dana they came up with a plan to end Bishop's existence without causing too much chaos in the streets.

Bishop already thought that Des was behind his missing product so it wouldn't be too far-fetched for people to believe that Des would kill Bishop and steal everything. Bun and Body had already put Des out on the streets as a man not to be trusted because of his interaction with CMM and Bishop. No one knew that Des was dead but Bun, Body, and Dana. So, this would turn out to be the perfect plan; if things ever get heated they could always blame it on a dead man.

Body quickly removed himself from the van with everyone else following his lead. He pulled his gun out of his waist band, checked his clip and cocked it to ensure he had one in the chamber. The four men moved in the direction of the old ice factory. They found no trouble entering as the door was unlock and slightly open. They were all on high alert as they moved through the factory with their weapons drawn and ready to kill anything that moved. They moved swiftly towards the back of the factory to an area that was dim lit. Body reached the enclosed area and was welcomed by yet another open door.

The room was set up like an office. Under the desk on the floor was a tiny LED light that gave the space just enough light to understand the surroundings. On the desk, sat ten stacks of money and one package wrapped in duck tape. On the floor next to a chair, sat a black duffle bag. Bun picked up the empty duffle bag and notice on the handle was the infamous CMM logo. Body snatch the bag from Bun, glanced at the logo imprinted on the bag and instantly, rage began to build inside of him.

This only confirmed what he already knew and what the plug, Julio, told him. Bishop was behind that setup that left his cousin, Ace, dead. Bun grabbed the bag back and began to fill it with the content that sat on the desk. After a quick search of the factory the men only recovered the money and the package left in the office.

"I want that nigga head fa real?" Body said as he entered the driver side of the van.

"Be easy my dude, Dana got us. That nigga good as dead," Bun said trying to somewhat put his brothers mind at ease.

"I hope that ol'bitch ass nigga die a slow painful death. I wanted to look into that niggas eyes as he takes his last breathe, but instead I gotta leave my dirty work to a bitch."

"Dana ain't no ordinary bitch, she a killer; she got us. Trust the process my dude."

"Bet that shit up."

# Chapter 11

## Eyes Wide Open

Dana, Bishop, and Kandi laid in bed as they were panting and catching their breath. The three had a stick of the best weed in rotation as they lay naked in their own juices. Bishop laid in the middle of the women with Dana to his left and Kandi to his right. Bishop left arm was underneath Dana while his hand gripped her ass. Kandi rested her head on Bishop's chest while Dana propped her head up with her right arm.

Bishop took a long drag of the blunt before passing it to Kandi and looking over at Dana.

"You sure know how to treat a nigga. I hope you giving me some more of that tight lil pussy before you go," Bishop said while exhaling smoke directly into Dana's face.

"I don't know if you deserve another trip to pink paradise," Dana said, while giving Bishop a seductive look.

Bishop placed a firm grip on Dana's ass and placed his other hand around her neck. Dana bit down her bottom lip and matched Bishop's energy by choking him too, but only with a little more pressure so that he could feel her strength. Surprisingly, it looked as if he was enjoying it.

"I told you I'm in charge, so stop trying to put me in check. I'll give you what I think you deserve, do you hear me?" Dana said while getting onto her knees, but never letting her grip go from around Bishop's neck.

Kandi sat up on the bed, anxious to see this play out. She was surprised at how Bishop melted to

Dana's touch and listened to her speak to him in such way. Kandi was used to Bishop controlling any and everything around him. Seeing him being controlled was a sight she did not want to miss.

Dana straddled Bishop while still choking him and still talking shit, "Tell me you want this pussy. Matter of fact, beg for this pussy."

"Put that pussy on me, please beautiful."

Dana could feel Bishop's manhood growing on her ass cheeks, but she was not finished dominating him.

"I wanna hear you say my name and I just might give you some."

"Dana! Dana! Dana!"

Dana's nipples tingle at the sound of her name. "That's right, say my name."

"Dana! Dana! Dana! Please pop that pussy for a real one."

"A real one huh," Dana said while reaching down and positioning Bishop to enter her. Dana slowly worked her vagina onto Bishop's massive dick. Bishop began to feel all of Dana's wetness on him as his face showed how good she was making him feel. Bishop's face looked like he just won the lottery.

Bishop reached up and cupped one of her full breast into his hand. He let his fingers massage her breast and nipple as he enjoyed her taking every inch of him into her wetness. He moved his hand slowly off her breast and placed it on her neck.

Dana bit her bottom lip and removed her hand from Bishop's neck and wrapped both hands around his arm of the hand that was wrapped around her neck. Dana picked up speed as she bounced her full round ass on Bishop's dick. Bishop's grip increased around Dana's neck as she continuously pleased him. Dana did not slow down giving Bishop all she had as she bounced and gyrates on his dick.

Bishop could feel himself about to explode, so he loosened his grip around Dana's neck and used his other hand to grip Dana's ass and pulled her up to remove her as he emptied his load all over her ass. Bishop let out two loud moans without fully releasing his grip from Dana's neck.

# Chapter 12

## Plug a Leak

Dana attempted to remove herself from Bishop's lap, but was stopped by Bishop applying pressure to her neck. The mood in the room shifted and immediately, Dana knew something was not right. She grabbed Bishop's arm and hand in an attempt to remove him from her neck.

Bishop began to laugh and said, "Bitches really think a nigga dumb."

"What?" Dana said while still trying to remove Bishop's hand from around her neck.

"I know exactly who you are! I been seen you coming since you took my people out back in Texas."

Bishop's grip got a little tighter.

"You are Bun's weak ass never noticed the camera set up on top of the cattle guard gate and, thanks to my bottom bitch Kandi, I knew all about that weak ass plan to send your fine ass to kill me while them bitch ass niggas run up in my shit."

Dana knew if she didn't think fast she would end up being the dead body left in this room when it was all over. From her peripheral vision, Dana could see Kandi sitting on the bed calmly as things between her and Bishop unfolded. She could barely breathe when she conjured up the strength to deliver a sharp and quick punch to Bishop's nose.

Bishop became instantly aggravated and gripped Dana's neck harder and flipped her onto the floor on side of the bed. He jumped up off the bed and sat directly on top of Dana's chest. All the air in her lungs escaped as Bishop applied all his weight to her chest. Right before she could attempt to catch her breath, Bishop placed his hands around her throat and continued to choke her. Blood from his nose dripped onto Dana's face as he finished talking to Dana.

"Them niggas stealing they own shit back. Sad when a motherfucker can't take they L and keep it pushing. All this over a nigga that couldn't even control his dick. Niggas die in these streets every day, that's why you gotta keep your heart out of business."

Bishop looked down at Dana with a look of admiration.

"Me fucking you was personal." He licked his lips and continued. "Me having to kill you is just smart business though. It's kinda fucked up for such good pussy to go to waste, but a bitch like you can take over an entire operation with ease, especially after what I saw. Kandi, get your ass off that bed. Get your blade bitch, and end this hoe."

Kandi reached under the pillow that she had previously laid on and pulled out an eight inch black blade with a chrome handle. Dana began to kick and scratching at Bishop's arm as he held his position on her chest. Kandi raised the knife in the air as she removed herself from the bed and stood over a kicking Dana with a smile. Kandi came down with force and entered the blade deep into Dana's abdomen. Dana let out the loudest scream she could.

Bishop looked down at Dana's face with pleasure as he watched her suffer and life slip from her eyes.

"I'ma watch the grim reaper swallow ya ass whole bitch," Bishop said as he tightened his grip and the fight in Dana slowly faded.

Bishop was enjoying feeling death at his finger tips, but for him, Dana didn't suffer enough for the trouble she caused and the money she made him lose out on. Bishop would not be satisfied until Dana's breath was one of pure pain.

"Kandi, poke this bitch again, and this time, make it nasty for Daddy," Bishop said while slightly releasing his grip from Dana's neck to let a little life inside of her so she could feel Kandi's blade.

Bishop heard no movement behind him. So he screamed Kandi's name while he remained seated on Dana's chest. Bishop took a glance back and could not see Kandi anywhere in the dim lit room.

"I know this bitch didn't get sick on me. Kandi! Kandi bring your stupid ass here. Don't make me come get you, because if I get up from her, I promise, it's gonna be two dead bitches in here."

Kandi ran back into the room and immediately began to apologize to Bishop as she quickly wiped her mouth.

"I'm sorry Daddy you know how I get when you punish people."

"Suck that shit up and do what I asked you to do, so we can drag this bitch body to the dump," Bishop said as he focused his attention on Dana's face so he would not miss the moment when Dana's face expressed the pain she felt from Kandi's blade entering her flesh. Bishop smiled as he looked down at Dana and said, "Go pop that pussy for the Devil bitch".

As soon as the last word left Bishop's lips, he fell on Dana like a ton of bricks.

"Dana!" Kandi said as she hurried to move Bishop's unconscious body off of Dana.

"Damn! Reaper if this nigga Bishop didn't kill her, you sure did! Come help me move this nigga off my girl. Thanks for having my back. I knew that nigga Bishop would have seen straight through that dumb ass plan we put together. That's why it's always good to travel with a shadow," Kandi said while already pushing on Bishop's body in her attempt to remove him off of Dana.

Reaper put his gun back into his waist band and helped Kandi free Dana from the weight of Bishop with ease.

"Damn, my dude, what do you do on your spare time, pick up houses?" Kandi asked as she hurried to check Dana for a pulse but couldn't find one.

"Fuck! Fuck! Fuck! She's dead!" Kandi said while looking up at Reaper.

"I know death when I see it Kandi. Drag her outside and call Body and Bun," Reaper said in his calm deep raspy voice.

Kandi pulled Dana's lifeless body from the side of the bed and headed toward the door.

"I can always count on you to get us into some shit, Dana," Alissa arose out of her space and spoke to Dana as pain gripped her and Dana's body and death slowly made an entrance.

As tired as Kandi was, she did not stop dragging Dana's body until she reached the garage. As Kandi laid Dana's motionless body and dialed Bun's number as Reaper requested, she was suddenly startled by gun shot that rang off inside the house. Shortly after, Reaper walked out the house with a designer back pack on his back and carrying a black duffle bag.

"I see you found the stash with no problem, I see," Kandi said to Reaper, but he didn't even pay her any attention. Reaper kept his stride and disappeared into the night without even sharing another word with Kandi.

Kandi had a short conversation with Bun, letting him know her location. Minutes after, a dark colored cargo van pulled up. Body and Bun exit the van and approached Kandi and Dana. Bun entered the house with his gun drawn while Body tends to Kandi and Dana.

As Body approached Kandi and Dana, Kandi said, "She's dead, Body. I didn't make it in time to save her. I'm sorry." Kandi stood up and continued talking to Body.

"I set up this shit with Reaper shortly after the night you'll kidnapped me from the club. Bishop was going to kill me because he already knew that you'll had a female stepper and that she single handedly took out Des. We needed a new plan if we still wanted Bishop dead."

"Nice looking out fam," Body said with his arms folded in front of him while he looked Kandi in her eyes. "We gotta get baby girl outta here, Kandi."

"I'll help you out. I thought maybe I should come with you guys anyways."

Bun was exiting the house as Kandi bent down to help out with moving Dana's body. He pushed Kandi to the ground, aimed his gun and fired one shot that landed in between Kandi's eyes.

"I guess the bitch forgot what happens to a leak," Bun said while walking past Kandi's body as if he never just ended her life.

"A leak gets plugged, my brotha. Now come help me move baby girl so we can take her home. We can't leave her like this," Body said while motioning for Bun to help him move Dana's body to the van.

Body and Bun carried a lifeless Dana to their van while being hidden by the night sky. The two men completed their mission with one great loss to their team. Even though the men only knew Dana for a short time, she was already family. Without her, justice would have never been served for Ace.

The men carefully placed Dana's body inside the van and closed the door. After getting inside of the van, the men traveled in the direction of one of Body's many stash houses as they talked about plans on how to give Dana a final goodbye.

"It's never a dull moment with you," Alissa said to Dana as darkness surrounded them. All Dana could do was laugh.

# Special Thanks

Thank you to anyone that took the time to read my creation, blessings to you and your love ones. Special thanks to my mom, Caroline Phillips, without you there is no me. Thank you for your love and support. I would also like to thank Carolyn Ayers for believing in my writing enough to help me give it to the world. Thank you to my real life Bun, Body, and Money also my oldest brother John, I am my brothers' keepers I love you guys beyond words. Thank you to my queens that always fix a sisters crown when we don't have the energy to do it ourselves. Love, peace, and power my beautiful black queens.

# Meet the Author

Hello beautiful people, as you may already know my name is Jonnie Patterson (Dauphine). I borrowed that Dauphine last name, but that's a story for another book. (Wink Wink) I from a small town in southeast Louisiana and I'm one of five children. I love my dogs King and Reine way too much and I have a strange addiction to composition books. I've always had a love for writing and creating things with words. Writing for me is like an escape, I can be anywhere when I'm writing and I really hope you guys enjoy the content I deliver. In the future I know my writing will bring me to new heights and I hope them heights have me in the same room as Tyler Perry. Trust me when I say the best is yet to come!!!

**Don't forget to check out Dangerous Dana!!!!**

www.ingramcontent.com/pod-product-compliance
Lightning Source LLC
Chambersburg PA
CBHW070747280626
47162CB00017B/2416